hungry ghost

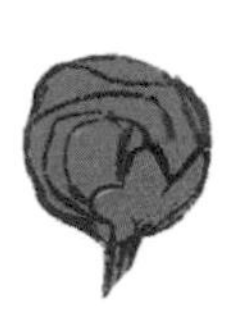

hungry ghost

Victoria Ying

Color by Lynette Wong

CONTENT NOTE:
This story includes depictions
of disordered eating.

PIZZA
For as long as I can remember, my mother always watched what I ate.

Happy Birthday to you...
...dear Valerie... Happy Birthday to you!
VALERIE

VALERIE

I have a special one for you.

Remember, don't eat,
just taste.

I always wanted to be gwai. There's no English translation, but it means *good* or *obedient*.

Thank you so much for inviting Jordan to the party.
Of course! It's never easy being new in town.

Yum!

Are you not going to eat that?
No, I'm...full.

I love cake! This one is great!

I'm like the Cookie Monster, but for cake!

Wanna be friends with Cake Monster?

Yeah!

Even now, I can still hear her voice every time I eat.

Yoink!

Hey! You shouldn't take Val's food, she might get even skinnier than she is!
Yeah, a stiff breeze'll take her away if you don't let her eat!

Yoink right back!

...and you just know that Mrs. Owens's quiz is going to be impossible.
Not for Val. She's a shoo-in for setting the curve.

Are you coming, Val?

Just a sec. I gotta make sure to get this perfect.

You and that lip gloss...

CLICK

CLICK

Nobody knows the truth.

hurrk

If I didn't do it, I'd have to eat less and people would notice. This way, I don't look weird.
Besides, I'm not thin enough for it to count. I'm not *dying*.

Je voudrais le pull en rouge.
Very good, Valerie.

It gets easier. It starts feeling pretty natural. No more uncomfortable than anything else girls do to be pretty.

TAP
TAP

Hey, Chu, can I borrow a highlighter? You're, like, the prep queen.

Oh, sure.
ZIP

You can keep it. I've got two in that color.

You're the best, Chu!

wink

Allan, are you drawing again?

Allan and I used to be best friends in elementary school. We would pretend that we were Voltron at recess.
But then he found sports, and it turned out he was really good at them.

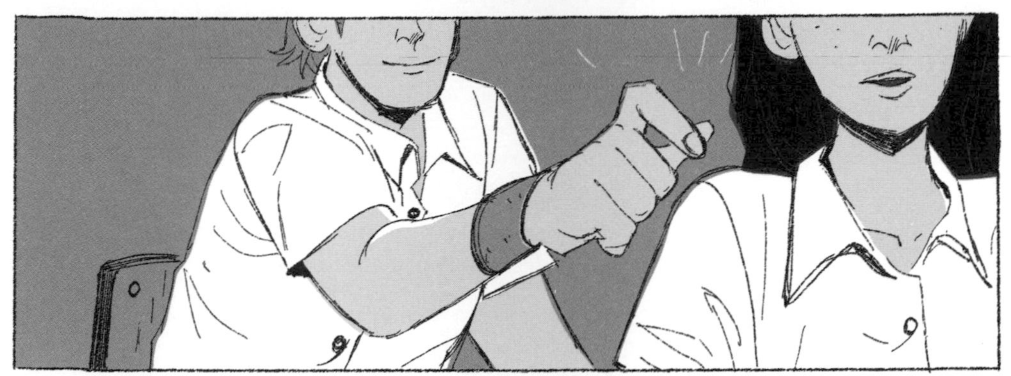

Hi!

And then I told him, "That's not what I heard!"

Oh my God, you didn't!

Sure did!
I'll text you later, and you can tell me more!

I'm home!

Ugh, such a shame about your friend Jordan.
What are you talking about?

When you get that fat, it's really hard to lose it.
All right, Mom.

Thank God
you're thin.

God has nothing to
do with it.

Kids!
Hey, Pops!
Dylan has been calling Dad "Pops" because of this manga series he started reading. It's weird. But Dad doesn't seem to mind.

Valerie, what are you doing? Set the table. Dinner is ready.

Mom's a great cook. I didn't appreciate it when I was little.

I used to be jealous of my friends, like Allan, who would get mac and cheese and pizza every night.

I didn't know how good I have it.

This looks amazing, Ma.

I thought I should make your favorites before you don't get to see a home-cooked meal for a while.
Dad travels a lot. Sometimes for work, sometimes for adventure travel.

Yeah, it's going to be weeks of granola bars and jerky on the hike.
Cut off the fat from that pork belly before you eat it.

I always have to try and be gwai.

CLIP
CLP

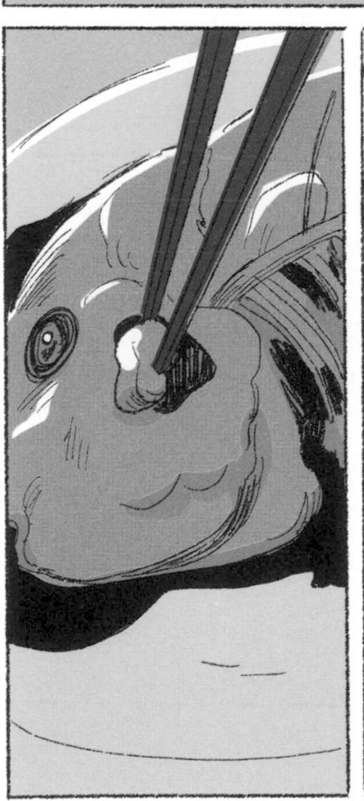

The best part for my little girl.

FLUSSHH

You never know if you really got rid of all of it. But it still manages to ease me. It makes me feel warm, comforted.

"Just taste."

scroll
scroll
scroll

I know I spend a lot of time looking at other people's bodies on the internet, but I can't help it. I see these girls, and my brain starts to try and see how similar or different I am.

Jordan
Yo yo brodie

What a do, boo boo.

Wanna grab some burgers with me and Allan?

Allan wants to hang out?

Sure. Pick me up?

Perfect. Cool, but not trying TOO hard.
Just like the girls on social media.

Bye, Mom, I'm going to the Fender Bender with Jordan.
But you just ate.

I'll only have a soda!
I always have to be good.

My mom acts like I don't ever think about what I eat.

But the truth is, I don't think about much else.

Are you guys ready for some deliciousness?
Always!

How are your folks, V? Dad still flying helicopters and riding motorcycles across volcanos?

Something like that. He's going to Tibet, climbing Everest.

Everest? That's crazy even for your old man.
It's not that crazy—it's a group expedition, and he's only going to Base Camp 1.

When we're like this, I could almost imagine that Allan and I are together, as if we are on a date, just the two of us.

Your dad tells the best stories!
Yeah, they're my favorite souvenir!

FENDER BENDER
I've been craving a milkshake all week.

Oh man, that and some fries would be brill.
"Brill"?

You're such a bran muffin. Brilliant.
Oh right, I'm the bran, not the girl making up her own language.

Hey, Allan, lend me a quarter?

Lend? Are you planning on giving it back?
Har, har.
MENU

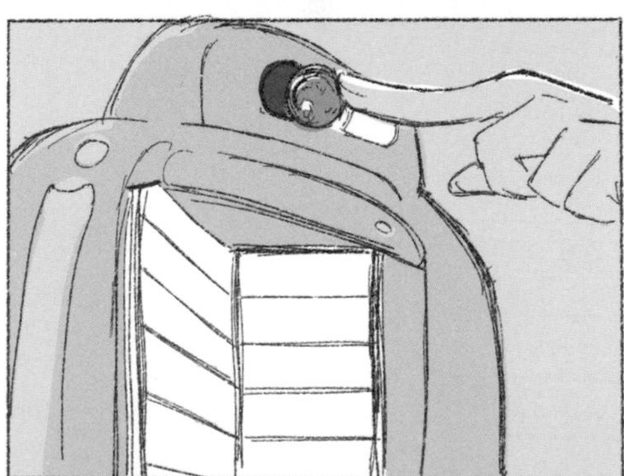

Val, you pick the song. Something... happy.

What would make Allan think that I'm smart and sophisticated?
flip
flip

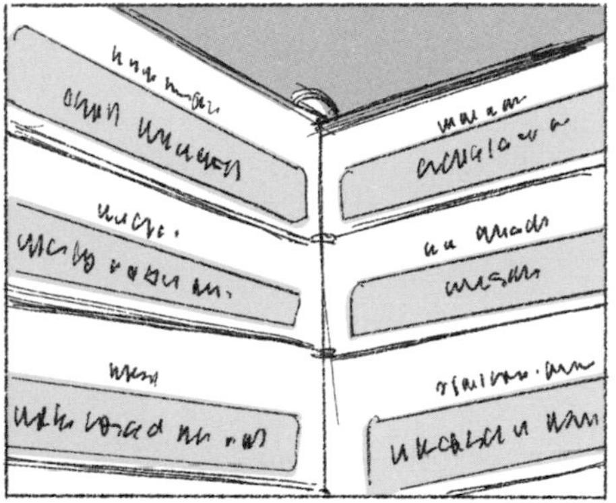

Oh, hey, Elvis! Classic!
My dad always sings this one at karaoke.

TAT
TAT
TAT
TAT

Trying out for band next year, Allan?
Naw, they couldn't handle these swift steps.
Good thing I purged. I'm totally empty now.

SLUUUURRP

Ooh, strawberry, can I try?

...Like an indirect kiss...

Anyways, I just figured it's been a long time since we've all hung out. I could use a break from the petri dish of testosterone from time to time.

Well, you came to the right place. We'll give you a healthy dose of feminine-goddess energy.
CLINK

HUFF
HUFF
HUFF
When I think about the food I eat, I literally feel sick.

I have to go to the bathroom!

Boys don't like fat girls...
HURK

If I'm ever going to have a chance with Allan, I'll have to be cool...

I'll have to blend in. Eat what everyone else eats, but still be thin.
Be good, look good.

Boys don't like fat girls.

Hey!
Oh, hi!
You down for some mochaccinos after school?

I can't today. It's Lunar New Year, so my family is coming, and I have to help get the house ready, cook...you know.

Man, I wish we had a holiday like that. Money envelopes every year must be sweet.
It is pretty sweet. And the food is always good, too.
Ah, I can just imagine it. Your mom's green onion pancakes...
DongPo Pork...
That awesome tofu thing?
MaPo Tofu.
Yeah! That! Maybe I'll get invited to a famous Chu dinner sometime soon!

DING DONG

Valerie, your face is looking bigger than last time! Have to be careful; don't get fat!
Good to see you, too, Auntie Shelby.

POKE

Valerie! You get prettier every time I see you.
No, Auntie Nikki, that's not true.

*Taiwanese slang for sister

Nights like this are the worst. I know I have to eat, but there are so many people around—who knows if the bathroom will be free when I need it? What if someone hears me?
So, Val, how are you doing? Have you sent out your college applications yet?
Not yet. I'm still picking schools.
I'm sure wherever you choose to go you'll do well. You're always such a good student.
Yes. Always good.

Don't forget to try some pig trotters! They're good luck! And the dumplings!

I never know what I'm supposed to do. How am I supposed to be good? Do I eat or do I not eat?

Is there cake?
Not this year. We have some watermelon for dessert instead.
Aww...
Oh crap, I forgot to count! How many calories was that?
Shit, shit, shit.

FLUSH

HSSSSSSS

Val, are you doing okay?

Shit, she heard me.

Yeah, totally good. I just... was feeling a little sick.

We should get back, or else we won't get any watermelon!

Maybe UCLA will be my first choice.
Oh! Me too!
UCLA

They've got a great law program, and those football players are hot.

Poor Jordan. She's my favorite person in the whole world, but a football player wouldn't look at her twice.

Berkeley would be cool, too.
Close enough to stay at home. Not a bad deal. Your mom's cooking is tits.

Never mention my mom and tits in the same sentence again.
Roger.

In my heart, I've always wanted to go to Sarah Lawrence College. Having lived on the West Coast my whole life, I want to see a real fall.

If you get into SLC, and I get into NYU, we can hang out on the weekends still!
As long as we finish and send these all off before Paris.

Oh, Paris! If I'd known freshman year that they do a class trip to *Paris,* I would have picked French over Spanish.
Oh, I'm sure we can make Mexico fun.

Crepes, baguettes, and macarons vs. tacos and margaritas? I'm not sure which one is the winner!

I am. Paris, for now and always.

We can't have the margaritas, so we're really just talking tacos.
One of the best foods in the world!
Best foods... Right, I'll just have to be extra careful when I purge...

Mmm...how about L'Estrella for a bite after class?

I'm in!
Me too!

I can't. I've got a "family meeting."

Another downer, eh?
SHRUG

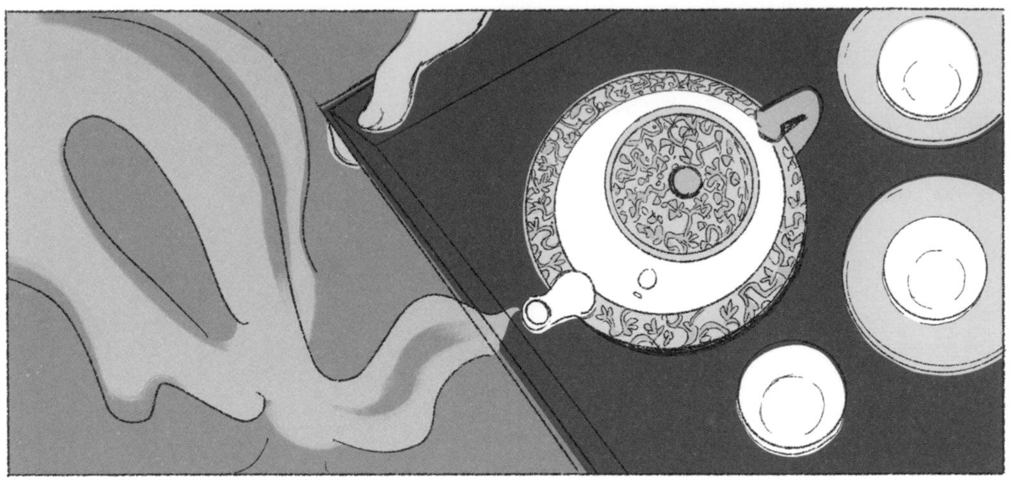

Dad calls meetings like this probably once a year.

As you kids know, the trip I'm about to take is risky.

I almost know everything by heart now.

Aw, Pops, we already know what to do... We know where to find the code for the safe... We know—
Dylan, put that away. This is important.

You need to hear it again.

Valerie, this is a copy of my will for you to take with you wherever you go to college next year. Just in case. Keep it somewhere secure.
NOD

Dad has always been very careful about this stuff. There's always a plan and a backup plan.
It shouldn't ever be necessary, but we want you kids prepared.

I know.

Sometimes, when he's away, I imagine what it would be like if we had to actually do the things that he asks.

But I guess none of us actually believe that anything bad will happen.

scroll
scroll
MISSYLEE
#PARIS

Everyone looks so beautiful in Paris. Standing against the Eiffel Tower. I hope to look like that, too.
LIKED BY RANDEEPK and 4,189
#PARIS #TRAVEL #
MINKYU Looks
such a

What about this? Do I look like a Parisienne?

Oh, definitely. All you need is a beret and a baguette over your shoulder.

Oh no, c'mon, girl. You know better than that. Mrs. Owens is going to have us trotting all over the city.
But they're so beautiful.

Not so beautiful if you're hobbling all over Paris like a newborn fawn.
Jordan doesn't understand. Being beautiful takes...work. It takes pain...and sacrifice.

All right everyone, make sure that you have your passports... your luggage...

Can you believe it? We're actually going to Paris!

Yeah! By this time tomorrow, we'll be in the City of Lights.

Très bon! Mes amis!

It's my first trip away from home without my parents.

The first time that I'll be with friends instead of adults.

The first time I'll be on a trip with a boy.

I can't wait to see the Musée d'Orsay.
Not the Louvre?

Well, the Louvre, too, but the d'Orsay has more of my favorite painters.
Allan is crazy talented. I can't even draw a stick figure. He's so sophisticated, too. What high schooler has favorite painters?

Maybe...he'll do a drawing of me.

I would love to go with you to the d'Orsay.
Yeah? We should all go! I know we'll be splitting into groups for some of the day trips, but it would be rad if you guys came.

It would be "rad," would it?

Sorry, I mean "brill."

Paris is the most romantic city in the world...

Who knows what might happen?

All right, everyone, I know that was a long trip. We're going to head to the hotel, and then we'll regroup for dinner. Rest, wash up, do whatever you need to do.

Everything already feels different.

Everything here feels so old.

It already feels magical.

I can't believe we're here!

The air even smells different.

It's because they don't pick up after their dogs.

PAFT

FLOOP
It's going to be like a whole week of sleepovers.
Yeah, except with Mrs. Owens and boys.

You mean Madame Owens and les garçons.

Ah, mais oui. Tu est ma petite amie.
You know that means "girlfriend," right?

I thought it meant "little friend?"
I'm not really that, either.

It's so beautiful.

And we haven't even gotten to eat yet!

CAFÉ
Now, students, I want us all to order everything today *en français*. Is that understood?

OUI, MADAME OWENS!

I could live here.
If I could find a decent taco, I could, too.

Have you noticed that there are a ton of carbs on these menus?
It's Paris, of course!

How do you think these women stay so thin?

Val, who cares?

Are they thin? I hadn't noticed.

Thin...and happy.

Our first real day in Paris!

All right class, we need to get a move on if we're going to stay on schedule!
Are you coming, V?

I have to...go to the bathroom.

TOILET
Never mind... I'll just go at the museum.

I can wait; I can do it. It will be fine.

CHATTER
CHATTER
CHATTER

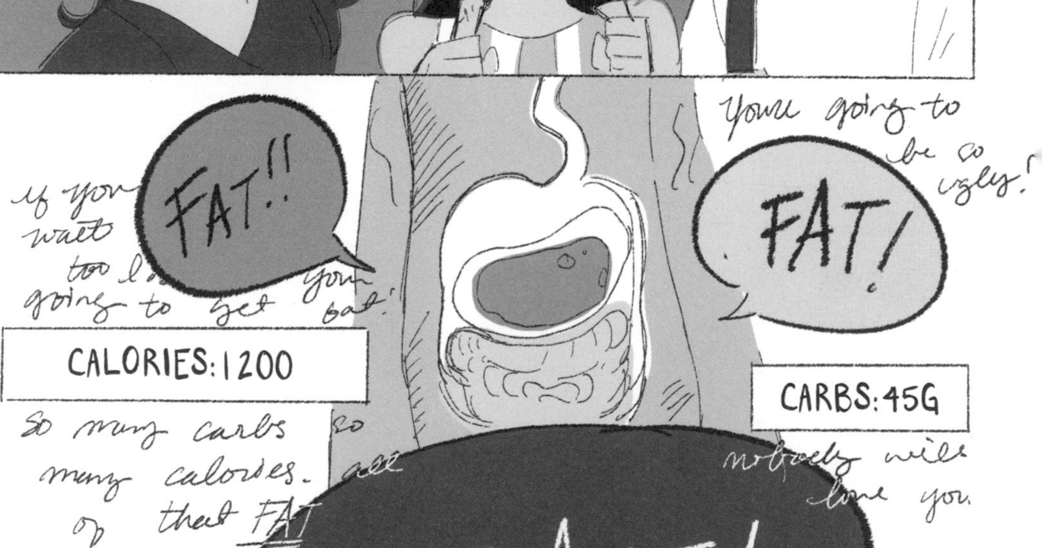
FAT!!
if you wait
going to get
CALORIES: 1200
So many carbs so many calories. all of that FAT
You're going to be so ugly!
FAT!
CARBS: 45G
nobody will love you.
FAAAT!

Hey, V, are you okay? You haven't said a word since we left the café.
I'm okay, thanks.
No, for real, V, you're looking kinda flushed.

You look like you've got a fever.

I'm fine!

Oh, hey, V!
I have this
painting I want
to show you!

I would love to see it.

It's my favorite.

It's very nice. Um, I like the gold.

Look at his use of pattern and color. She's so complex and beautiful.

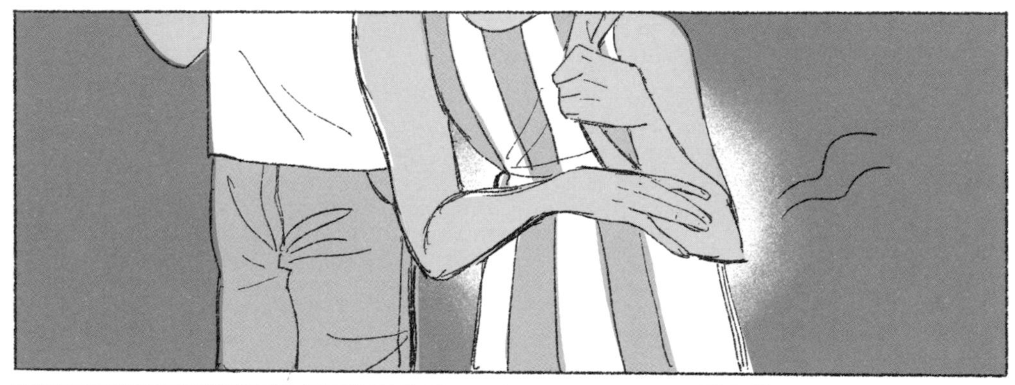

I have to go!
Wha—?

ZIIIIP

CLICK
hurrk
I hate that I had to do that...
We almost had a moment and I ruined it.

But what choice did I have?

Hey, are you okay? You don't look so good.

I'm fine. I just... had to get some air.

We've got a few hours before we need to meet everyone for dinner. How about you and me just do a little exploring?

But we don't have a map. What if we get lost? What if we get in trouble?

That's the idea. Let's go get lost, maybe find a little trouble.

I would
look fabulous
in that!

Yeah, you really would!

Oh! And that one for you!

Wow!
Yeah!

I should post this on Insta!

This is the best crepe I've ever had in my life.
No doubt about that.

Paris is pretty great, isn't it?

Yeah. It is.

Hi, dear, I saw your post on Instagram. I hope you didn't eat that whole thing.

Got it, stalker. What time even is it in San Jose?
I guess I'm failing at being good enough.

So, did you see all the paintings you wanted to see?
Yeah! I wish I could have shown them all to you. Where did you guys go?

Oh, we just got a little lost.

Jordan is so happy. She doesn't care that she's fat. It doesn't make her miserable.

WHACK

Why am I so afraid? Maybe it doesn't take being thin to be...happy.

Valerie...you are so beautiful.
KNOCK KNOCK

KNOCK
KNOCK

Valerie?

Wh— Um—
Yes?
There's something we urgently need to talk about.

While flying out to Tibet,
his plane crashed.
He was flying the plane himself.
It crashed. Shortly after takeoff.

He must have been so scared.
How could I have been so stupid? How could I have actually believed that he couldn't die?
My father is gone again... No, my father is dead.

If anything happens, it will all be okay.
I promised myself when I was young that I would live my life in the richest way possible.
I've done that every day, and if I were to die right here, right now, I would have no regrets, because I did it all.

My father died with no regrets.
I couldn't die now and feel like I have lived my life. I haven't.
I've lived like a prisoner to my body.
I wonder what he would say if he knew that? Maybe it's a good thing. He would be so disappointed in me. A daughter so unlike himself.

Does Mom know you're using her car?
She's asleep. Has been for the last couple of days.

I don't know what to say to my brother.
And it seems he doesn't know what to say to me, either.

WHUMMP

How are you?
I don't know. Not okay?
How's Mom?

Really, really not okay.

SQUEEZE

There's lots of food in the kitchen. People keep bringing stuff.
Thanks...
I'm not sure when Mom will be up. I've been trying not to wake her.
I'm glad you're back.
Me too.

I guess grief is supposed to make you hungry.
And for the first time, I just eat. The numbers, the math, none of it is coming to me.

sob
sob
sob

I got some condolences through texts from my friends in Paris, but it didn't change much.

Morning.
What's going on?

Dylan? Can you fit into this?

Maybe I
can grow into it.

We can give
away a lot of
the clothes—
But what are
we going to do
with these?

Mom, we should do this later...
No later...

SLIP

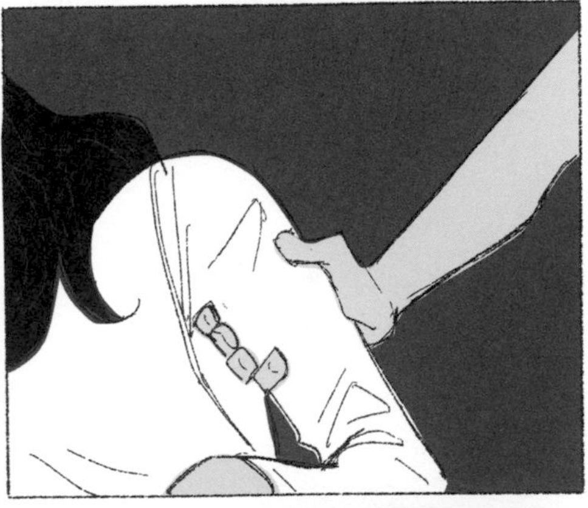

How long has she been like this?
Pretty much since it happened.

What's this?

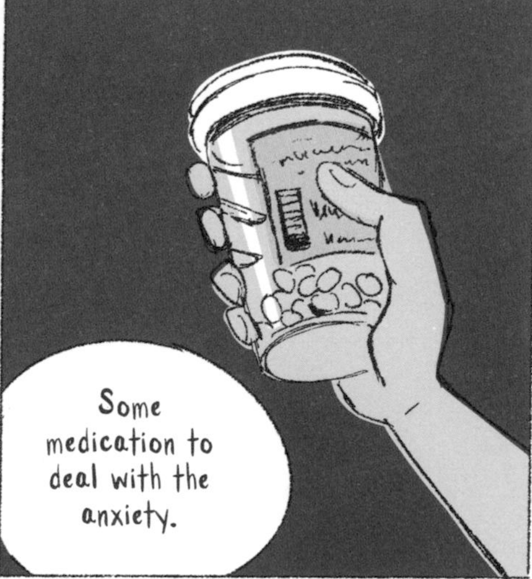
Some medication to deal with the anxiety.

Let's get some breakfast. I think the milk in the fridge is still okay.

Hi, this is Val reaching out on behalf of my mom. She's taking some visitors. We can have you visit either tomorrow or Thursday at 12 or at 3.

I haven't really been able to think too much about my dad.
I've just been trying to hold my mom together. Trying to be a good daughter.

I'm so sorry...
I can't believe it.

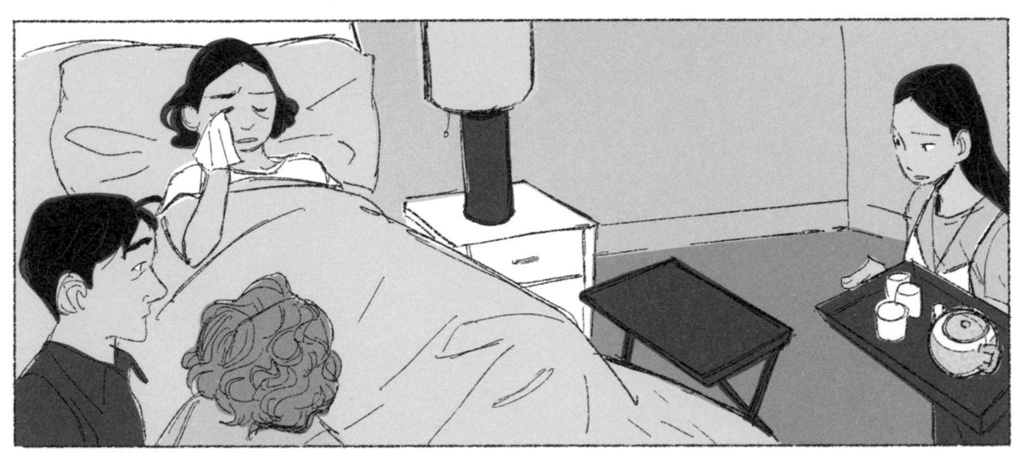

At least I tell myself that's why I haven't been able to think about my dad.

You can't leave me, Val. You need to stay with me.

SARAH LAWRENCE COLLEGE

Okay.
SARAH
I have to be good.

I understand that we have gotten the body from the coroner.
Yes, I want to see him.

I'm not sure that's advisable. The coroner said that he doesn't recommend—
I don't CARE!

My mom has been obsessed with seeing the body.
But I don't understand it. I don't want to see it at all.
My dad isn't in there anymore.
I want to remember him as he was.
Well, all right, you are allowed to, you just need to sign a liability waiver since you are going against advisement.

I want to be there for my mom.
I want to be a good daughter.
But I can't do this.

Are you ready?

Mom.

Mom, I can't. I can't do this.

But you have to. You have to say goodbye to your father.

I... I can't see him like that.

It's okay, Mom. I'll go with you.

Will people care that much about my body when I die? Am I my body?

How can this thing, this thing that I hate—how could anyone care about it that much?

How are you doing, Val? This must be so hard for you.
It's not easy, but we'll get through it.

SOB
SOB SOB

I can't imagine what my mom is going through. She never saw it coming. She never imagined, like I did, what it would be like to carry out his instructions...
I don't think he knew that this would happen to her. Or to us.
What a disappointment we all are.

Valerie, your brother is out tonight. It's just you and me for dinner.

Is this it?

We need to control ourselves. After all that food everyone brought over, I can see that you are gaining a little weight.
Mom...

Once you get fat, it's so much harder to get thin again. Like your friend.
With everything going on, I haven't been thinking about food...about my body. Maybe Mom's right...

Have I really gained weight? I haven't had time to think about it...
WHO CARES?

Special delivery!
12:01

I'm so happy to see you!

I'm sorry Allan and I couldn't be at the funeral...
It's okay! I missed you, though.

I know this won't make up for anything. But I thought we should get you lots of Parisian treats, so that at least you wouldn't have missed out on that stuff.

Ta-da!
These were my favorites!
They're even better than the ones we tried at the shop on the Champs. These are funny flavors like lavender and Earl Grey!
These are incredible, Jordan...

I saved the best for last.

I took Allan to the store and showed him the one you were looking at.
Allan painted this of me?
Yeah, I had to help him a little on the likeness—he forgot about your dimple.

Thank you, J. It means a lot to me.
Talented, isn't he?
Crazy talented.

Do you want to talk about what happened? How are you doing?

That's the last thing I want to talk about. It's like it's all I've been allowed to think about. Just tell me more about Paris...

Aw, it was just okay—you didn't miss much.
Jordan...c'mon, seriously, don't try and make me feel better!
Okay, okay! I mean, it was Paris! We went to the Eiffel Tower and Allan made me climb the whole thing.
Seriously?
I showed him. I beat him to the top by a whole ten minutes. He was huffing and puffing by the time he got there.
Ha ha!

You'll never believe what happened next.

What?

Ah! It's so crazy, I can barely believe it!

Now you have to tell me!

Allan kissed me.

Are you okay?
I... I...
What, what is happening? How...?

How, why...?

What's wrong, Val?
You guys... together?
Hard to believe, huh?

How?
How could he
pick you?
What?
Why you?
What are you
asking?
I think you
know.
Actually,
I don't.
WHY WOULD HE
PICK YOU OVER ME?
YOU'RE FAT!

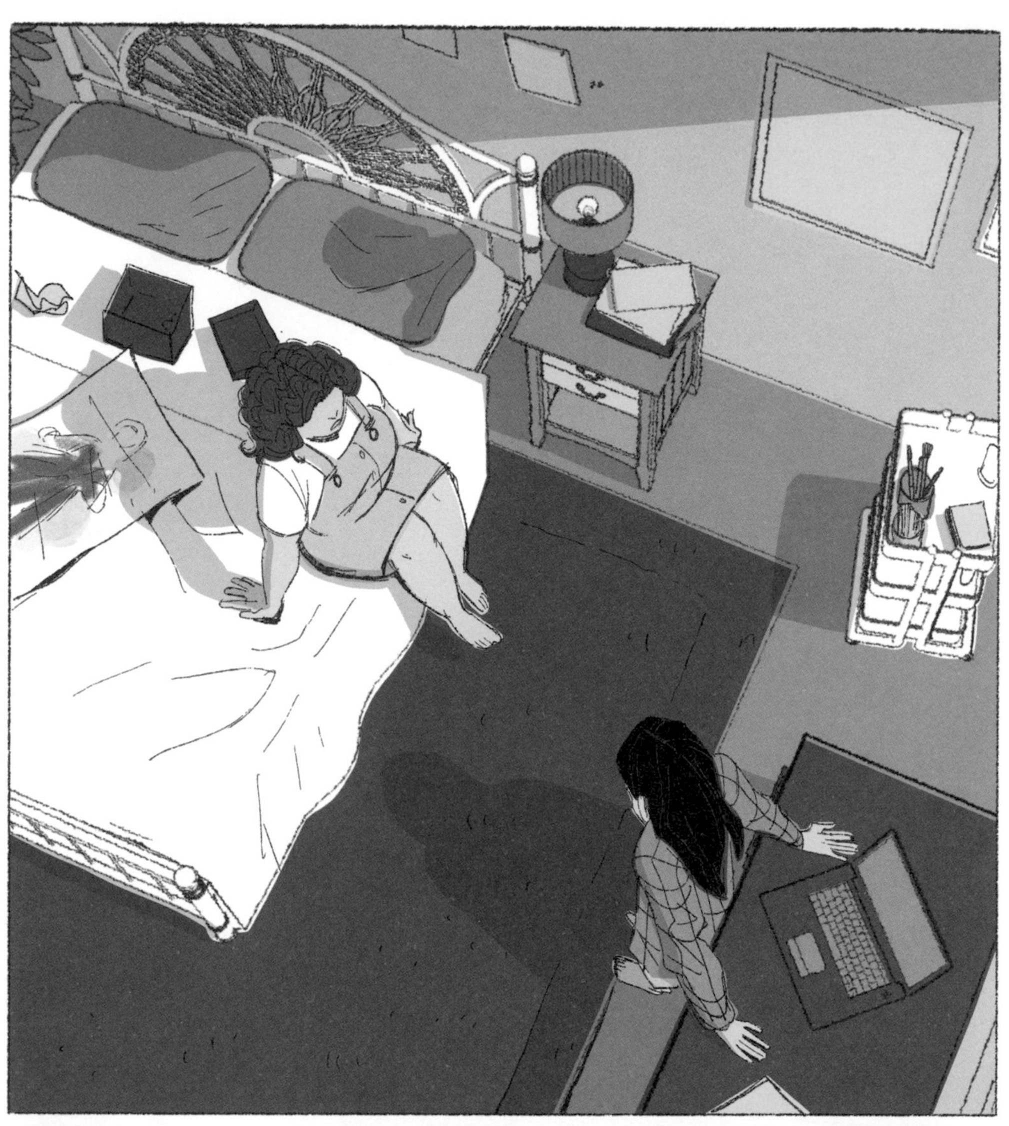

Over...over you? I didn't even know you liked him.

SLAM

I know you didn't mean that—

I did! Why? You're not pretty. Why would he like you?

Is that really what you think of me? Is that all you see when you look at me?

Not "my best friend, Jordan," not "my fun and funny confidant," you just see me as... fat and ugly?

That's sad. That's so fucking sad.

CLICK
SOB
SOB
SOB
SOB
SOB

The Langham is beautiful, an old hotel with lots of history. Mom wanted to come here for lunch, just the two of us.

Val,
I need to talk to you about something.
What?

What are you doing to stay fit?

Oh, you know, we have gym class.
TENSE

Have you ever considered giving up cheese? Or desserts?

No. I hadn't.
Well, I think that it could really benefit you to think about doing it. It's not that difficult.

But I don't want to.

Valerie, I didn't want it to come to this—

Come to what, Mom?

Valerie, I'm just worried about your health!

My "health"?

You know it's very unhealthy to be fat.

I'm not fat.
Well, not yet.

I can feel it. This fiery anger starting to boil up in me.

Why does it matter so much? Who cares if I'm fat?
Valerie, other people will judge you if you're fat.
Other people. You mean you?

I will always love you.

But you don't always accept me.

I just want the best for you!
Then want the best for me! For real!

It's because of that fat friend of yours—

Leave Jordan out of this!
I'm just saying! I saw what she brought you back from Paris.
Paris...

Jordan cares about me. She's a great person. The best person...

You were so thin before.

That's because I'm sick.

What? What do you mean?

I'm sick, Mom. I make myself throw up...

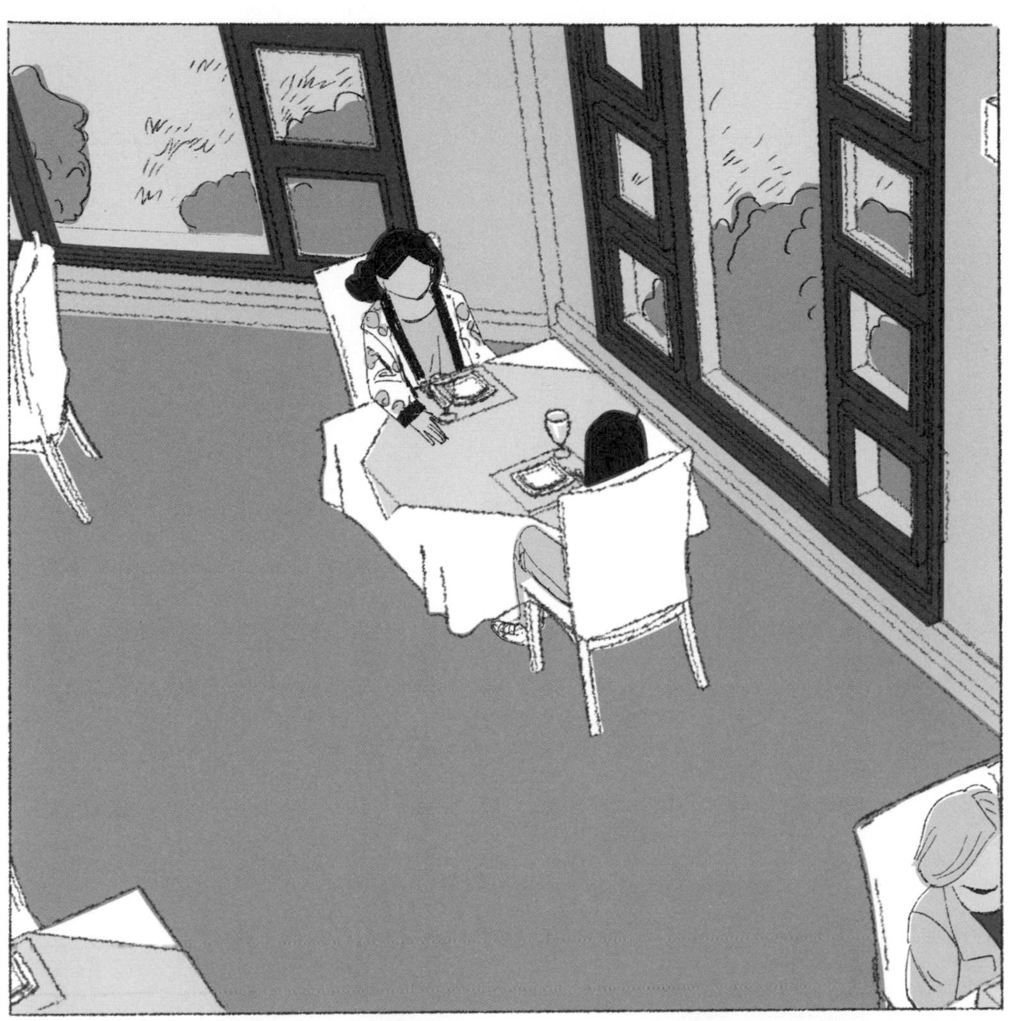

TRICKLE
TRICKLE

Well.

Why don't you just diet? Then you won't have to do that anymore.

You don't understand.

You don't have to do that— thing—to be thin. I just care about your health.

What about my mental health?

Just stop doing it and you'll be fine.

No, Mom, it's not like that. Why can't I be enough? Why am I not okay as I am?

I just want to make sure you don't GET fat in the future.
Stop.
Maybe just give up eating cakes.
STOP.
SCREECH

She doesn't even care. She doesn't care that I'm sick. That I could be dying. All that matters is that I'm thin.

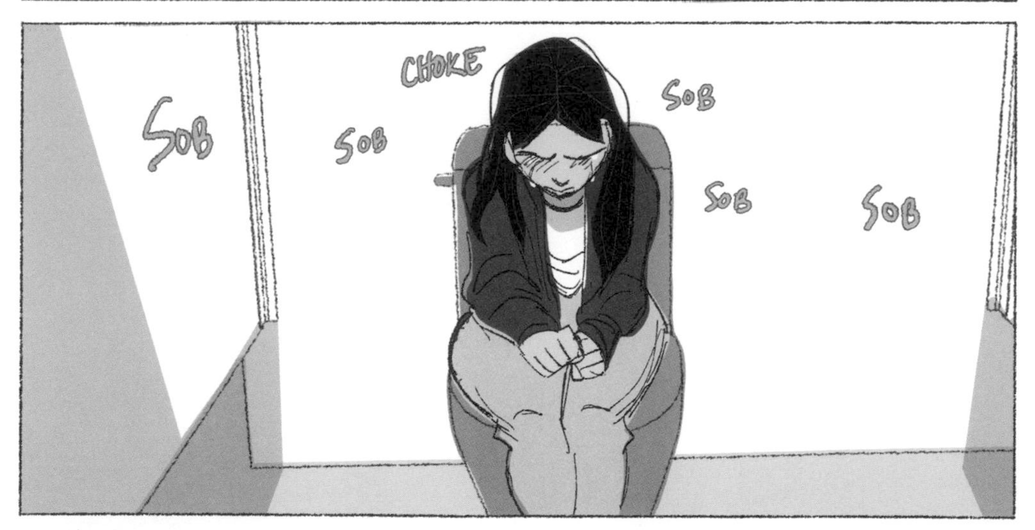
SOB
SOB
CHOKE
SOB
SOB
SOB

KNOCK
KNOCK

Hello?
Are you okay?

Yes, I'm fine.
Thanks.
I can't believe I was too stupid to lock the bathroom.

...

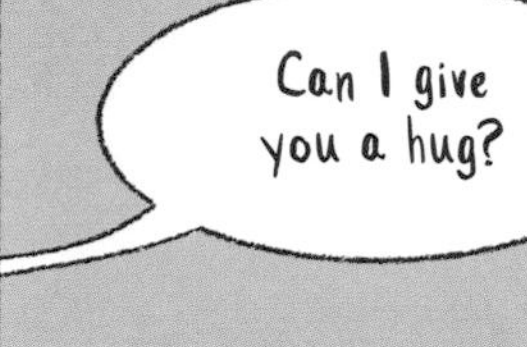
Can I give you a hug?

I overheard you and your mom.

She might not ever understand, and I just want you to know that you're beautiful.

0 new messages

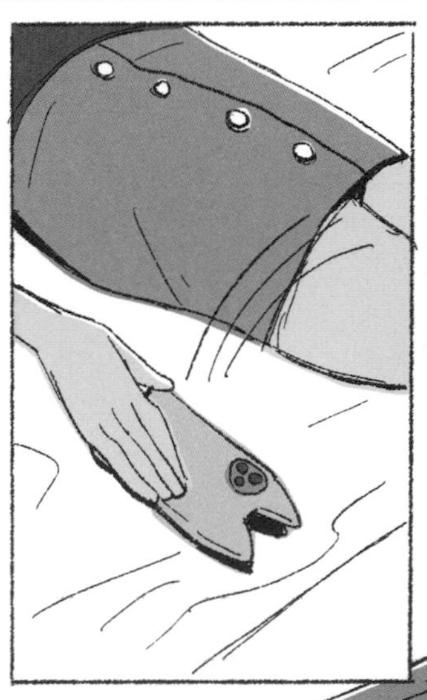

I've tried to reach out to Jordan. I tried texting her, but she hasn't responded.

Not that I blame her.

3
15

KNOCK
KNOCK
Yes?

How ya doin',
kiddo?

Aunt Nikki! I didn't know you were coming over.

I wanted to come and check on you all. I know things must be hard since the accident.

Dylan tells me that you haven't been coming out of your room for the past few days, even for dinner.
...

Tell me what's going on.

How did you do it, Aunt Nikki? How did you live with Grandma and Mom and everyone else and not end up...angry at them?
?

So this isn't about your dad?

I'm just so tired. I'm so exhausted thinking about food and Mom and my weight and—

I thought something was up.

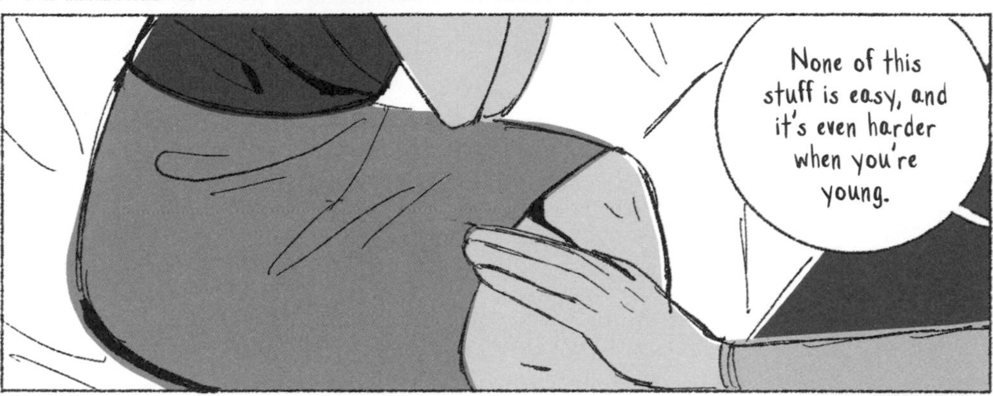
None of this stuff is easy, and it's even harder when you're young.

I feel like I'm empty inside. I feel anxious and sad and angry, and I'm so tired.

Your mom loves you. Just like Grandma loves me, too. But sometimes, they can hurt you more than they know.

CONGRATULATIONS!
SARAH LAWRENCE COLLEGE
Oh my God, you got into Sarah Lawrence! That's your top pick, right?
flop
Yeah, but how could I go? With Dad gone, Mom will be all alone.
You see, even though you are hurt, you still want what's best for your mom. That's what love is. Your mom loves you like that, too.

It's hard to admit when you've hurt someone that you love.

I think she might not ever really understand. But I can tell you that she doesn't mean it.
She's doing her best to love you the way she knows how, and her best maybe just isn't enough. But you can't rely on her to change.

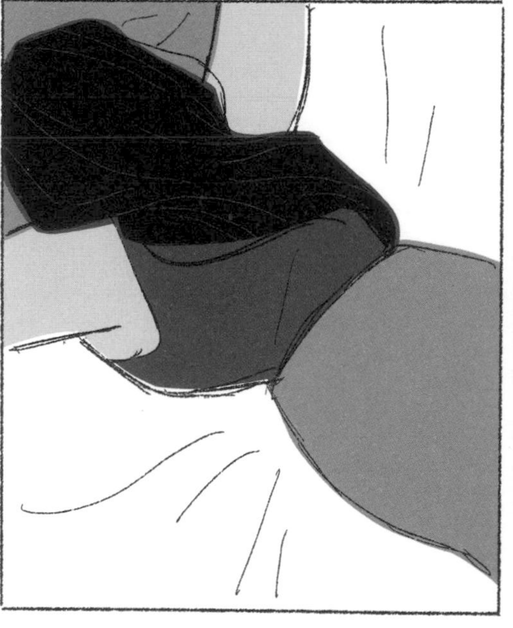

You can't rely on her to be enough for you. No one ever is. You have to find your own way to be happy. Whatever that means.

Love yourself the way that you want her to love you.

But there's so much about myself that I hate.

What makes you say that?

I'm a bad friend.
Just try to be better. Do your best. Like your mom is doing her best.

What if it's not enough?
All you can do is try.

Hey. My mom said you were out here. I didn't tell her about what you said, but I'm not sure I want to talk to you.

Jordan, I...
I'm—
I'm so sorry for the hurtful things I said to you.
You mean so much to me.

Of course Allan likes you. He likes you for the same reason I love you. You light up a room.

You make everyone around you better. I'm so sorry.

You know—
for the record—
I didn't even
know that you
liked Allan.
No, that's not
it at all. I'm tired of
being so selfish. You
deserve to be happy.
You both do.

That was a really
craptastic thing you said to me.
I haven't been able to stop thinking
about it. I'm still really,
really pissed at you.

I know.
I think it's the worst thing I've ever said or done in my whole life.
I guess it's nice to find the bottom.

I think I would rather have let that stay a mystery.

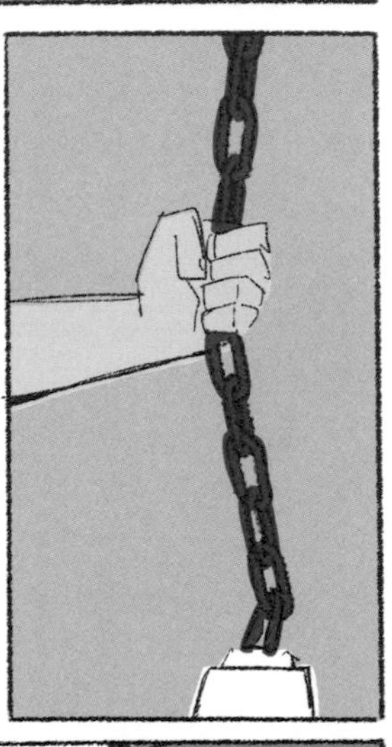

You think this will hold?
Of course.

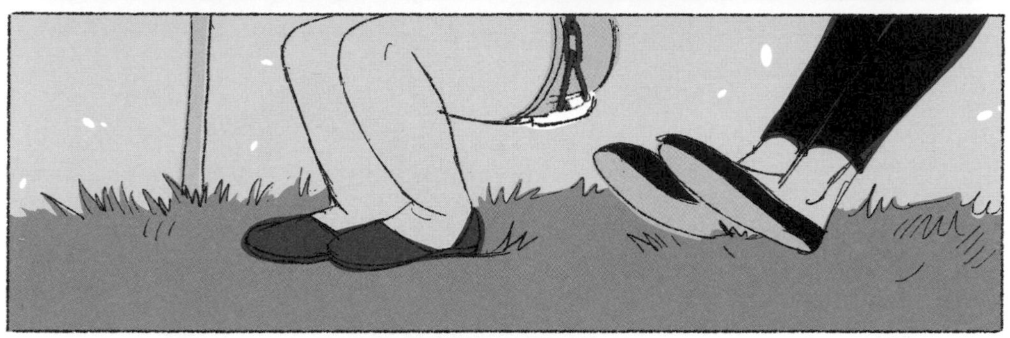

Remember when we were kids and we would always try to go over the bars?
Yeah, I never got as high as you. I was always too scared.

Are you still scared?

SKIIIID

Yeah. I am. Jordan, I have something to tell you.

What is it?

GRIP

I—I don't know how to say this. It's really hard for me to hear myself say it. But you're my best friend. You really are, and I need to be able to tell you.

You can tell me anything.

I'm sick. I—
I make myself throw up.

I said those awful things because the truth is that I hate myself. I hate the way I look, and I hate that I can't stop.

I'm sorry.

You don't have to be sorry. If anything, it's thanks to you I even saw the light at all. I thought you had to be thin to be happy, to be loved.
The truth is, it made me so self-centered. I couldn't see you or him. I was so obsessed with my body—I was so blind to everything else.

But...but you showed me that it just takes being happy with yourself. I can't thank you enough.

We'll get you better. Together.

How'd it go?

It's a start. It's weird having this secret for so long and just...talking about it. I had no idea there were so many people going through the same thing.

Does your mom know where you are?

No, but that's okay. I don't need her to know. Thanks for helping me find it. I was too scared even to search for it online.

Hey, you did plenty yourself. You found that eating disorder support group at your new college all on your own.

Mom! I'm home.

Hi, Jordan, Valerie. Do you guys want some fruit? I cut it up for you.

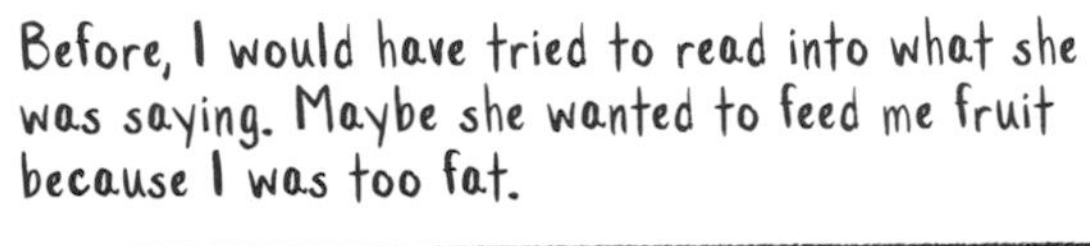
Before, I would have tried to read into what she was saying. Maybe she wanted to feed me fruit because I was too fat.

But now, I can see it for what it is. It's just food.

Sure. We're going to go upstairs and get started working.

I can't wait to visit you in the city. We've got lots to make up for after Paris.

Yeah, let's get lost again.

No, I'm not better.

And I don't know if I'll ever really be totally better.
But I can be a better friend.

I know that I can at least try. I can let myself be happy. That part is my choice.

I never thanked Allan properly for the painting. It's beautiful. I'm going to hang it in my dorm room.

You can tell him yourself.

What do you say? One last hoorah at the Fender Bender before we drive up?
Absolutely.

Let me finish up this box and I'll be rightdown. You can go ahead.

All right, I'll find us some good tunes.

It's your favorite...

Pears...
Thanks, Mom.
Remember not to eat too much when you get to school.

I know she loves me, even though she doesn't know how to help.
My version of being good is being good to myself.

I'll take care of myself. I promise.

There are parts of me that still feel bad for leaving. But I know I have to do it. I need to get better. Mom may never understand, but it's okay. I'll understand. I'll love myself, and I'll love her, too.

I love you, Mom.
I love you, too.

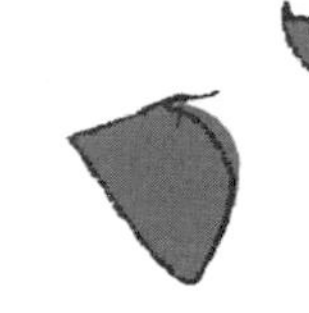

ACKNOWLEDGMENTS

This book could not have been possible without the support of so many people in my life. First, my agent, Jen Azantian, who read my book and connected with it on a level that I couldn't have dreamed of. My cheerleader from draft to sub and publishing.

To my editors, Calista Brill and Kiara Valdez, whose gentle and encouraging guidance was invaluable to crafting this story.

A special thank you to my husband, Patrick Laffoon, who read the very first draft and encouraged me to tell this hard story.

To my best friends, Bonnie, Lily, Georgia, Devon, Kim, Kate, and Julie. Thank you for listening to me whine about this book.

AFTERWORD

Val is not me, but I was her.

Writing this book was a challenge. And yet it wasn't. I wrote this at a time in my life where I was tired. So tired of waiting until I was thin to be happy. It was hard to write because it was raw, but it was easy because it flowed out of me from my brain straight through to my keyboard and through my pen.

It wasn't until my early thirties that I considered myself fully recovered from disordered eating. It took me a long time, but reading books like this nudged me down the right path. It's hard when everything in our culture tells us thin is better, thin is ideal, and thin is healthy. What's not healthy is obsessing over food and restricting your calorie intake to fit a perceived ideal.

I write fantasy, but this story was as real as it gets. I never thought I would make something like this in a thousand years, but the way it came to me almost fully formed, I could not deny it.

I wanted desperately to be seen and understood by those around me, and it took me years of reading memoirs, seeing therapists, and working my way through my own brain to find a way to just be happy for myself. My happiness shouldn't be sacrificed at the alter of thinness. I punished myself for every way I was failing, and all it did was keep me trapped in an endless cycle of torture and disappointment.

When you have an eating disorder, all you can think about is food. First in the eating of it, and then in the guilt around having eaten it. It's an exhausting state of being.

I freed myself by letting go of any expectation for my body to fit the cultural ideal. I chose to be free, and I've never been happier.

RESOURCES

Here are helpful resources, but please keep in mind that some of these may be triggering while in recovery. If you need more support, seek help from registered dietitians who specialize in Health at Every Size

Anti-Diet by Christy Harrison

The Body is not an Apology by Sonya Renee Taylor

Hunger by Roxane Gay

The Intuitive Eating Workbook for Teens by Elyse Resch

Maintenance Phase (podcast) by Aubrey Gordon and Michael Hobbes

Unbearable Lightness by Portia de Rossi

What We Don't Talk About When We Talk About Fat by Aubrey Gordon

www.nationaleatingdisorders.org

Published by First Second
First Second is an imprint of Roaring Brook Press,
a division of Holtzbrinck Publishing Holdings Limited Partnership
120 Broadway, New York, NY 10271
firstsecondbooks.com

Library of Congress Control Number: 2022908851

First edition, 2023
Edited by Calista Brill and Kiara Valdez
Cover design by Kirk Benshoff
Interior book design by Molly Johanson and Yan L. Moy
Color by Lynette Wong
Production editing by Sarah Gompper
Layouts in ComicDraw, Inked in Procreate, Colored in Photoshop.

Printed in Malaysia

ISBN 978-1-250-76700-4 (paperback)
3 5 7 9 10 8 6 4 2

ISBN 978-1-250-76699-1 (hardcover)
1 3 5 7 9 10 8 6 4 2